Jeanne Willis   Tony Ross

OLD DOG

ANDERSEN PRESS

"We don't want to visit Grandpa!" whined the Young Pups.

"He's so boring. All he ever does is talk about the olden days."

"And he has dog breath," they whimpered.
"And he keeps scratching himself."
"And he slurps when he eats."

"Grandpa is very kind though," said their mother.

"Kind of stinky!" snorted the Young Pups. "Kind of scary!"

"His bark is worse than his bite," said their mother.
"Oh, he can't bite!" howled the Young Pups. "He hasn't got any teeth."

Even so, the Young Pups were made to visit Grandpa!
He was thrilled to see them.

"In the olden days ..." he began.
"He's off again!" yawned the Young Pups.
"When I was young ..." said Grandpa.

But nobody wanted to listen.

The Young Pups played amongst themselves.
They played new games that Grandpa didn't know.
"You don't play it like that!" they yapped.

"Grandpa can't keep up," they said. "He's living in the past. Oh well, you can't teach an old dog new tricks."

"I wasn't always an old dog," snapped Grandpa.
"I've had my moments."

But they didn't believe him.

Grandpa went indoors.

"He's gone for a snooze," they said.
"He's gone to rest his weary old bones."

Soon after, Grandpa called them in.

He was wearing a ruffled collar, a clown's hat
and a sparkly waistcoat.

"Grandpa's not himself," they yipped.
"He's barking, the poor old stick.
It's time he went into a home."

"I know what you're thinking," growled Grandpa. "I wasn't born yesterday. Give me that ball. Fetch me that bike."

"Stand back!" he said. "Watch this, you young whippersnappers. You might learn something."

Grandpa balanced the ball on his nose.

He did a wheelie on the fence,
and cycled along it . . .
at top speed . . .

on one leg . . .
juggling eggs . . .

in a blindfold . . .
whilst whistling.

It was an old trick, but it worked.

"Bow-Wow!" said the Young Pups.
"Where did you learn to do that, Grandpa?"

"In the olden days when I was young,
I ran away to the circus..." he began.

And this time, they let him finish.
In fact, they wouldn't let him stop.

"Tell us again, Grandpa!" they begged.
"Please can we stay longer?"
"Please will you teach us to do tricks?"

Grandpa very kindly
agreed ...

"Go, Grandpa!" panted the Young Pups.
"See?" said Grandpa.

"There's life in the old dog yet!"